For my ever-jolly father

— Haynes Brooke

To three very merry girls — Suzanne, Maddi and Charlotte

— Jimmy Holder

Diamond Street Publishing
203 Diamond Street
South Pasadena, CA 91030

Book design by Jimmy Holder
The text of this book is set in Marker Felt
The illustrations in this book were rendered in Procreate

Printed in the United States of America

Library of Congress Cataloging-In-Publication Data
Brooke, Haynes; Holder, Jimmy
Santa Swallowed A Fly

p.cm

Summary: In this rollicking take on the classic rhyme, Christmas itself is at stake this time! Why, oh why, did he swallow that fly?

ISBN 978-1-66780-691-4

{1. Santa_Fiction. 2. Christmas_Fiction. 3.Reindeer_Fiction. 4.Adventure_Fiction.}

SANTA
Swallowed A Fly!

By
Haynes Brooke

Illustrated by
Jimmy Holder

One Christmas Eve, Santa swallowed a fly.

I don't know why he swallowed a fly.
Santa's not normally that kind of guy.

To smush the fly, he swallowed a shoe.

It stuck in his jelly-roll belly like glue.

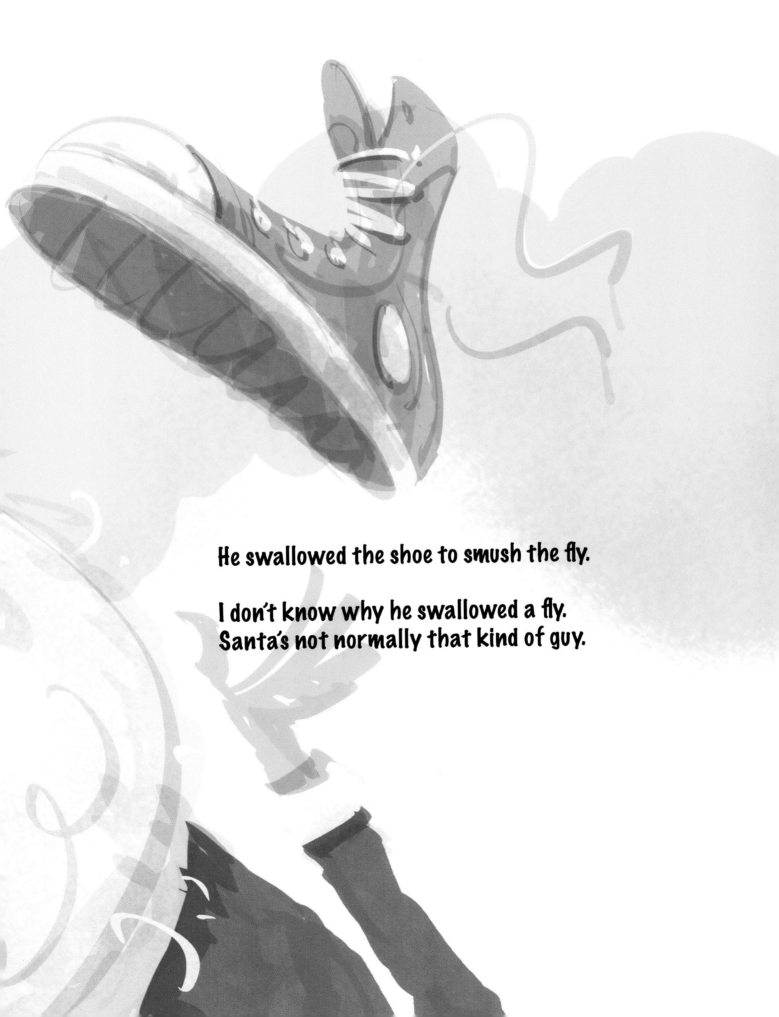

He swallowed the shoe to smush the fly.

I don't know why he swallowed a fly.
Santa's not normally that kind of guy.

To nudge the shoe, he ate bells that jingle.
Not exactly what you would expect from Kris Kringle.

He ate jingling bells to nudge the shoe.
He swallowed the shoe to smush the fly.
I don't know why he swallowed a fly.
Santa's not normally that kind of guy.

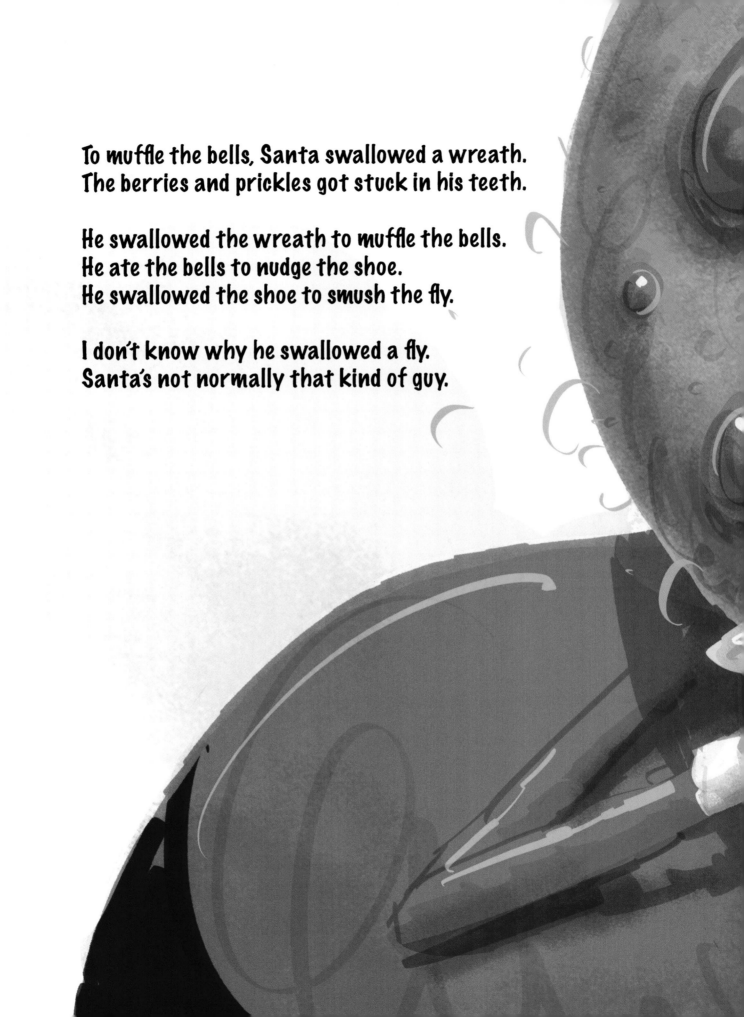

To muffle the bells, Santa swallowed a wreath.
The berries and prickles got stuck in his teeth.

He swallowed the wreath to muffle the bells.
He ate the bells to nudge the shoe.
He swallowed the shoe to smush the fly.

I don't know why he swallowed a fly.
Santa's not normally that kind of guy.

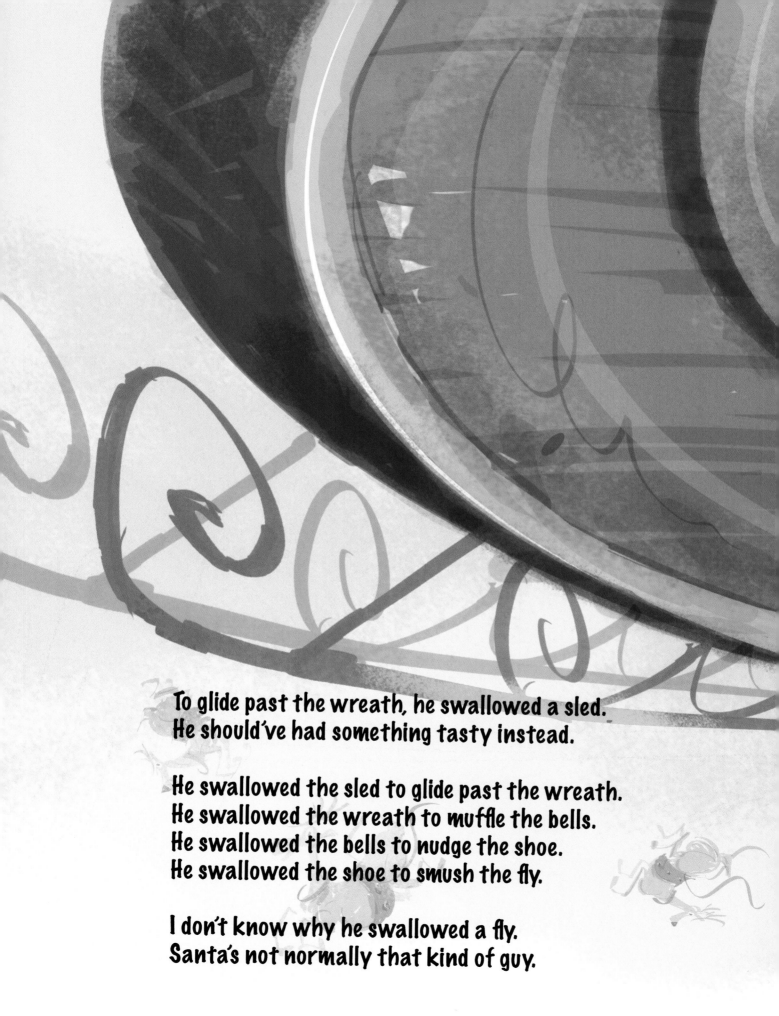

To glide past the wreath, he swallowed a sled.
He should've had something tasty instead.

He swallowed the sled to glide past the wreath.
He swallowed the wreath to muffle the bells.
He swallowed the bells to nudge the shoe.
He swallowed the shoe to smush the fly.

I don't know why he swallowed a fly.
Santa's not normally that kind of guy.

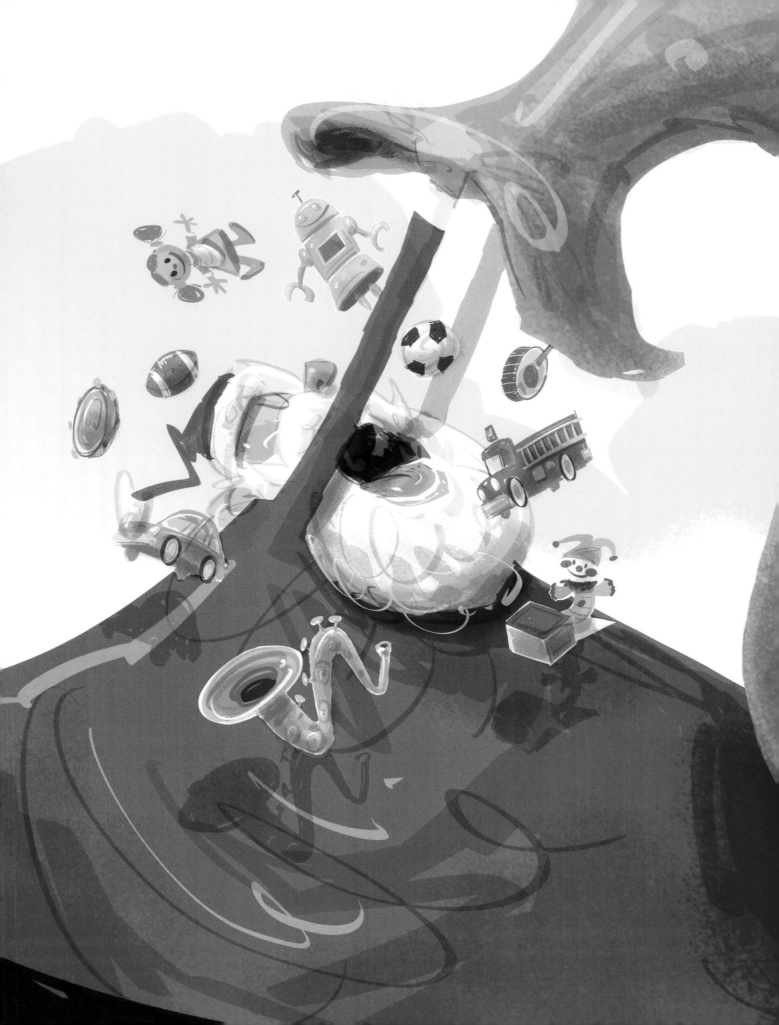

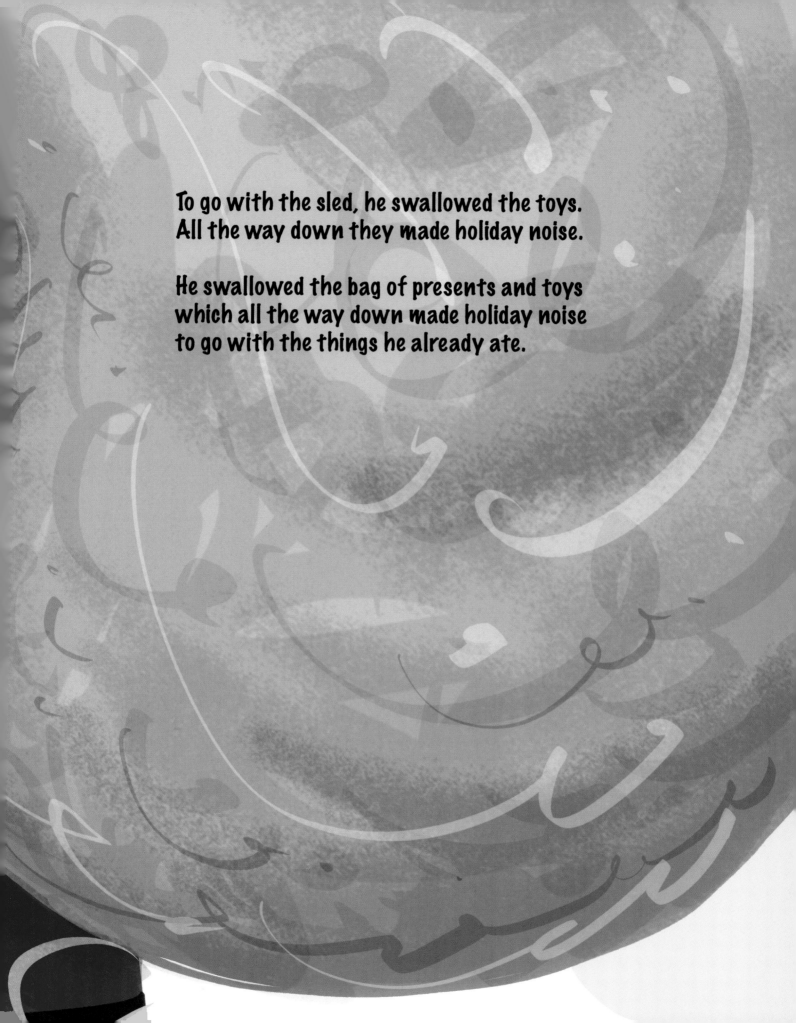

To go with the sled, he swallowed the toys.
All the way down they made holiday noise.

He swallowed the bag of presents and toys
which all the way down made holiday noise
to go with the things he already ate.

To be honest, at this point he didn't feel great.

And that is when Mrs. Claus quietly spoke.
"Time to wake up, dear."

And Santa awoke.

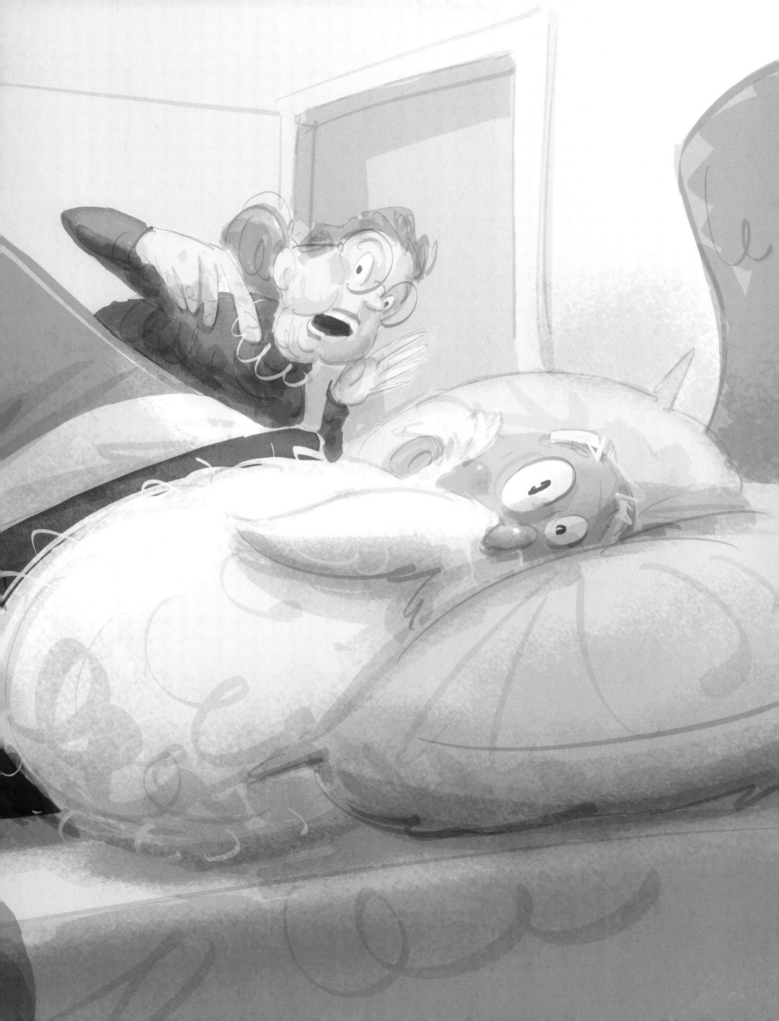

Good heavens, my dear! The dream I just had!
I swallowed a fly!

"Oh my, that sounds bad."

To smush the fly I swallowed a shoe
which stuck in my jelly-roll belly like glue.

"An unusual thing for a Santa to do."

To dislodge the shoe, I ate bells that jingle.

"Not exactly what I would expect of Kris Kringle."

To muffle the bells, I swallowed a wreath.
But the berries and prickles got stuck in my teeth.
To glide past the wreath I swallowed a sled.

"You should have something tasty instead."

To go with the sled, I ate all the toys!
And all the way down they made holiday noise!

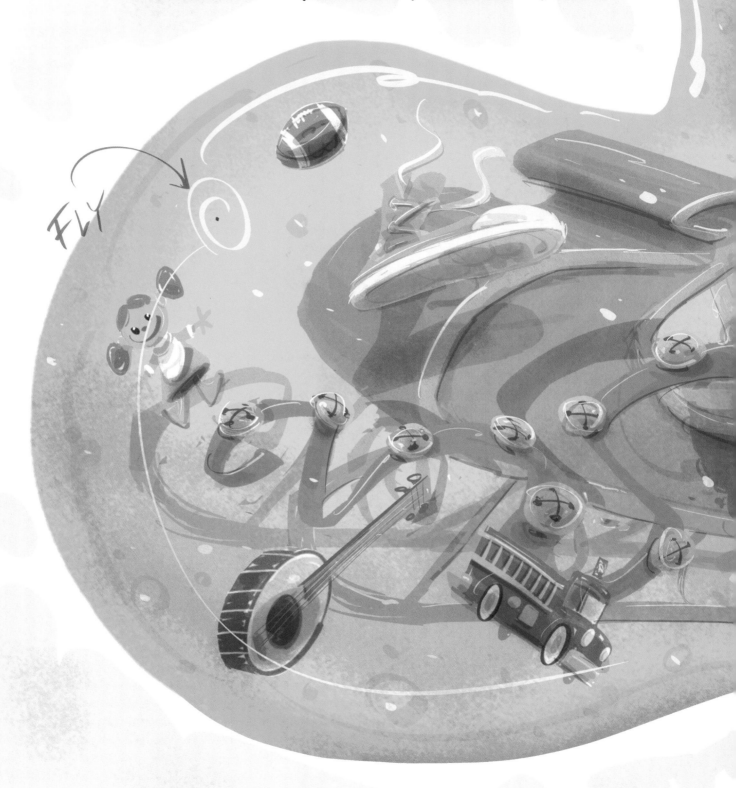

I ate the toys to go with the sled,
I swallowed the sled to glide past the wreath,
I swallowed the wreath to muffle the bells,
I swallowed the bells to nudge the shoe,
I swallowed the shoe to smush the fly,

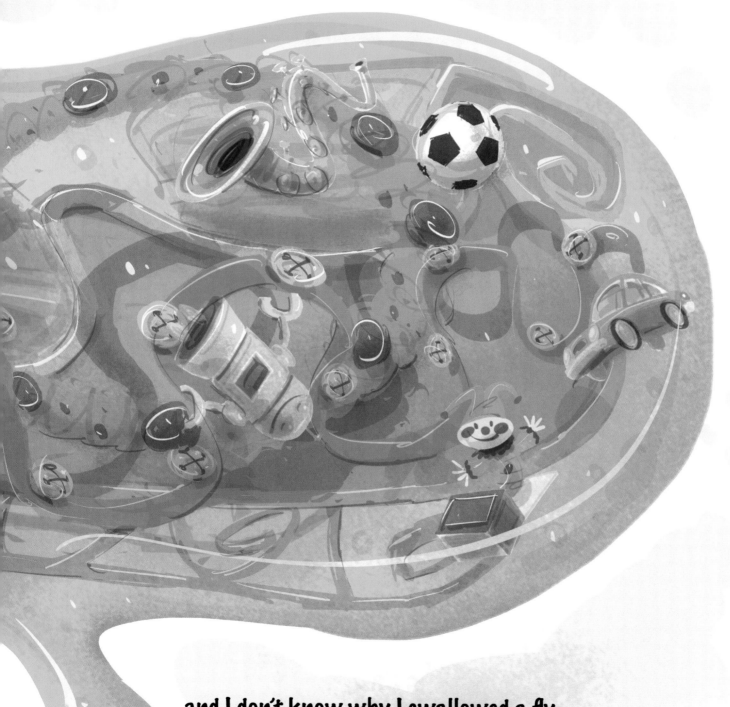

and I don't know why I swallowed a fly.

"Santa, my dear, neither do I!"

But now that I see it was all just a dream,
why don't we all have...

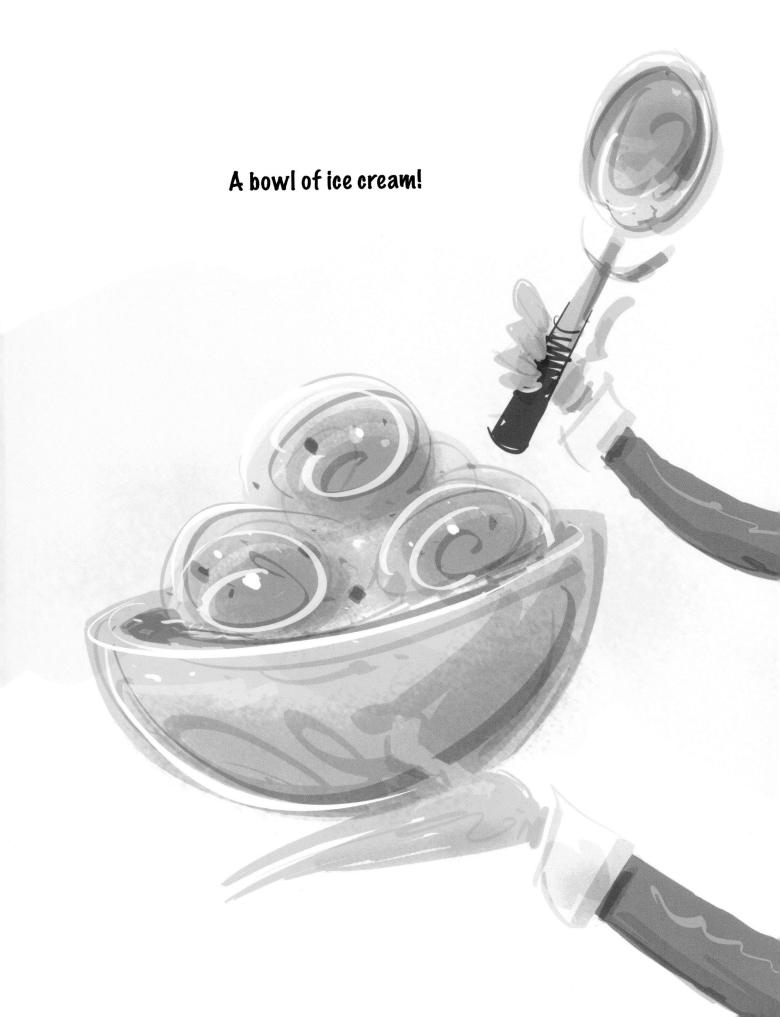

A bowl of ice cream!

He served them all ice cream, and I'll tell you why:

Santa Claus, he is just that kind of guy.